Hans Christian A...

Thumbelina

and other fairy tales

D0131569

Miles
KeLLY

First published in 2015 by Miles Kelly Publishing Ltd
Harding's Barn, Bardfield End Green, Thaxted, Essex, CM6 3PX, UK

Copyright © Miles Kelly Publishing Ltd 2015

2 4 6 8 10 9 7 5 3 1

Publishing Director Belinda Gallagher
Creative Director Jo Cowan
Editorial Director Rosie Neave
Editor Amy Johnson
Designers Rob Hale, Joe Jones
Production Manager Elizabeth Collins
Reprographics Stephan Davis, Jennifer Cozens, Thom Allaway

All rights reserved. No part of this publication may be reproduced, stored in a
retrieval system, or transmitted by any means, electronic, mechanical, photocopying,
recording or otherwise, without the prior permission of the copyright holder.

ISBN 978-1-78209-756-3

Printed in China

British Library Cataloguing-in-Publication Data
A catalogue record for this book is available from the British Library

ACKNOWLEDGEMENTS
The publishers would like to thank the following artists who have contributed to this book:

Front cover: Ag Jatkowska (The Bright Agency)

Inside illustrations:
Thumbelina Christine Battuz (Advocate-art)
The Farmyard Cockerel and the Weathercock Ayesha Lopez (Advocate-art)
The Travelling Companion Martina Peluso (Advocate-art)
The Snail and the Rose Tree Kristina Swarner (The Bright Agency)

Border illustrations: Louise Ellis (The Bright Agency)

Made with paper from a sustainable forest

www.mileskelly.net
info@mileskelly.net

Contents

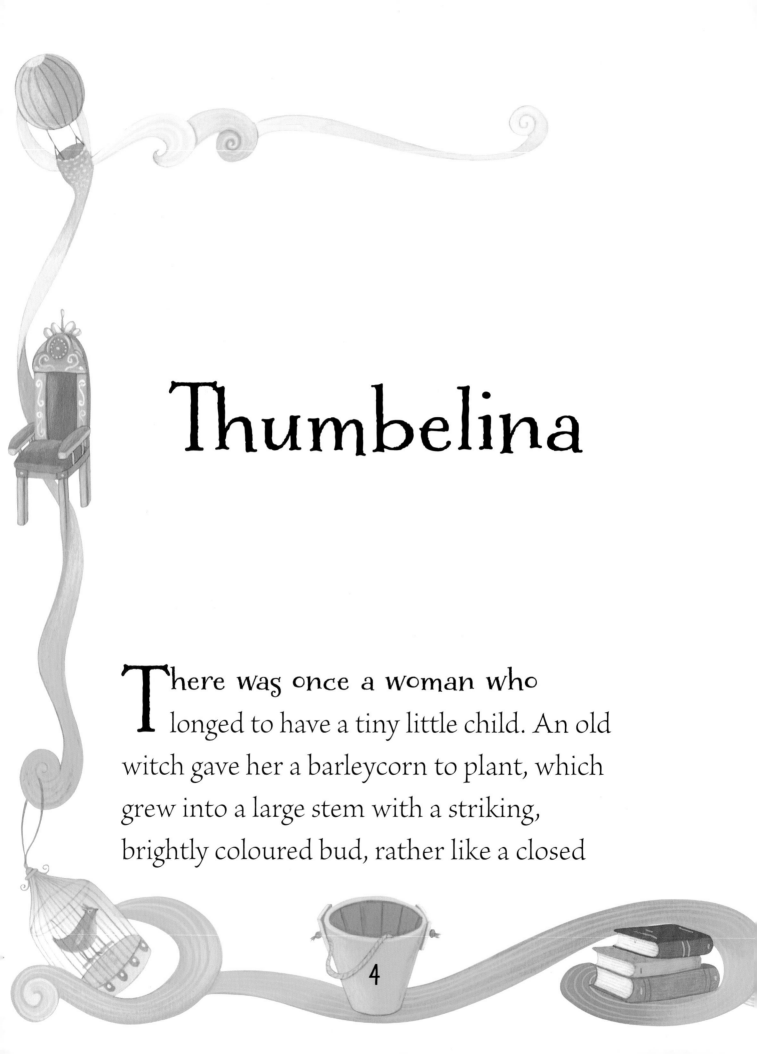

Thumbelina

There was once a woman who longed to have a tiny little child. An old witch gave her a barleycorn to plant, which grew into a large stem with a striking, brightly coloured bud, rather like a closed tulip. The woman kissed its red-and-yellow petals and – *POP!* – the bud opened. In the middle sat a tiny girl, no taller than a thumb. So the woman called her Thumbelina.

Thumbelina was enchanting. She was dainty and beautiful, and when she sang, she had the sweetest voice ever heard. In the daytime, she liked to float on a dish of water in a tulip petal boat, and paddle back and forth. At night, she slept in a bed made of a polished walnut shell with a rose petal quilt.

One night, a horrid old mother toad came hopping in through an open window. The creature looked at the sleeping girl and thought, 'Here's the perfect wife for my son.' She picked up the walnut shell and hopped off with Thumbelina, out of the window and into the garden. A broad stream ran through it, and so the mother toad swam out into the middle of the water and laid the walnut shell, with Thumbelina still sleeping in it, upon a flat water lily leaf.

The next morning, when Thumbelina awoke and found she was a prisoner on a little island, she began to cry bitterly. In the mud across the water, the mother toad and her son sat, scooping out a new home for him to live in with Thumbelina.

Thumbelina sank down on the water lily leaf, sobbing. She did not want to marry a toad and live in a nasty swamp.

The little fishes who lived in the stream

popped up their heads at the sound. How sorry they felt for Thumbelina! They decided they would try to help her, and so they all gathered around the water lily stem and nibbled away at it. Soon, it was gnawed in two. Away went the leaf, swept off down the stream.

Thumbelina drifted along in the sunshine, happy to be far from the toads. A lovely butterfly fluttered around her and came to rest on the leaf. Thumbelina undid the sash from around her waist and fastened one end of it to the butterfly, tying the other end to the leaf. That way, she could travel along even faster.

Just then, a big beetle swooped down and

grabbed Thumbelina, and flew off with her into a tree. She was very frightened, but the beetle was kind to her. He set her down on a large green leaf and told her how pretty she was – until all the other beetles arrived.

"What do you mean, she's pretty? She's only got two legs!" scoffed one.

"She hasn't got any feelers!" said another.

"She looks like a human being – really ugly," sneered a third.

Then the beetle changed his mind about Thumbelina. He picked her up again and flew down out of the tree. He left her sitting on a daisy, crying.

All summer long, poor Thumbelina lived alone in the woods. She wove herself a

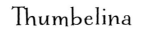

hammock of grass beneath a big burdock leaf for shelter. She ate honey from the flowers and drank the morning dew.

But then the winter came. Snow began to fall and Thumbelina shivered with cold. The big burdock leaf withered with all the other plants and flowers, and Thumbelina had to search for new shelter.

In a nearby grain field she came across a little field mouse, who was very kind and took pity on Thumbelina. "You can live with

9

me in my house," the tiny creature said. "All I ask is that you keep my house clean and tidy and tell me stories, for I love stories."

So Thumbelina did as the field mouse asked and she was comfortable and content.

A few days passed and the field mouse's friend, Mr Mole, came to visit. The mole was totally charmed by Thumbelina. He didn't really know how pretty she was, because he couldn't see very well, but he was bewitched by her sweet voice. He invited Thumbelina and the field mouse to come and visit him whenever they wanted.

Thumbelina didn't want to go underground, but the field mouse insisted. So a few days later they set off through the tunnel to Mr Mole's house. They had got halfway when they came across a dead swallow on the ground. Thumbelina was sad and wondered how he had come to be there.

All the time Thumbelina was at Mr Mole's, she couldn't stop thinking about the poor swallow who should have been out in the open air, in the winter sunshine. That night she crept back down the tunnel with a little coverlet to spread over him. She bent and kissed him… and heard a soft *thump, thump,* as if something were beating inside his chest. It was the bird's heart! He was not dead, only numb with cold. Thumbelina hurried to fetch him some water and soon the little bird was revived.

"Thank you, thank you," he gasped.

Thumbelina looked after the swallow in secret all through the winter. Then, when spring arrived, Mr Mole announced that he was going to marry her. "You are lucky," the field mouse told her, "for he is very rich."

But Thumbelina wept as though her heart would break. She could not bear the thought of living underground, never to be out in the warm sunshine again.

"I am strong enough to leave now," the swallow told her. "Climb on my back and I will take you away with me."

"Oh yes, please!" said Thumbelina.

So up they soared, over forests and lakes and mountains, far away from Mr Mole and

the darkness of his underground home.

At length they came to a warm country, and a blue lake in a magnificent garden, where there was a palace of dazzling white marble. "Choose one of the flowers in the garden," said the swallow, "and I will put you down in it to rest."

Thumbelina chose one of the loveliest large white flowers. To her surprise, in the centre of it there was a little man with bright shining wings, wearing a golden crown. He was the spirit of the flower. There was a spirit living in every flower, but he was king of them all.

Thumbelina and the flower king fell in love with each other at once. They were soon

married, and the best wedding gift was a pair of wings for Thumbelina, so she could flutter from flower to flower just like her husband. Everyone rejoiced – especially the swallow.

The Farmyard Cockerel and the Weathercock

Once upon a time, there was a cucumber growing in the vegetable patch of a farmhouse. She was wondering who was the most useful – the handsome farmyard cockerel or the weathercock that sat on top of the farmhouse roof.

The cucumber pondered over the question for a long time. Then she decided: "I suppose it has to be the farmyard cockerel who is more useful. After all, he wakes everyone up in the morning with his proud *cockadoodledoo*. But the weathercock can't even creak, let alone crow. The weathercock doesn't have hens, nor chicks, he just sits up there and thinks of himself.

"Yes, the more I think of it, the answer has to be that the farmyard cockerel is best. Every step he takes looks like a dance! Every *cockadoodledoo* sounds like music!" And so the cucumber rested in the vegetable patch, content with her decision.

That very night, there was a terrible storm. The wind howled loudly and rain lashed down. The hens, the chicks, and even the farmyard cockerel trembled as they sheltered in their wooden houses.

However, even though the weathercock was at the top of the farmhouse roof, in the thick of the storm, he sat firm. He did not even turn round, because he was old and had become stiff and rusty through spinning to tell the wind direction for so many years. He just sat with his head held high in the black storm clouds, and was lit up every now and again by bright flashes of lightning.

Next morning, when the sky was clear and the sun was out, the little birds all came out of their hiding places to go swooping and diving through the air.

"How silly they all are," muttered the weathercock as he watched them fluttering here and there. "The pigeons are fat and only think about filling themselves with food. The swallows are good at telling stories of all their adventures in warm foreign lands, but they say the same ones over and over again – they get boring after a while. And those thrushes can't stop whistling – it gets on my nerves!"

The weathercock did not want to be friends with any of the little birds. "The world is no good," he grumbled. "Everything in it is just stupid."

Then the cockerel and the hens and chicks

19

came strutting into the farmyard. "Cockadoodledoo!" the cockerel crowed. "My chicks will grow up big and strong, just like me." And the hens and chicks clucked and chirped. "What a champion of cockerels I am!" he crowed, and with that, he flapped his wings and made his comb swell up.

"That farmyard cockerel is stupid too," the weathercock said to himself. "What is he good for? He can't even lay an egg!"

But then there came a mighty gust of wind and the weathercock snapped right off. His rusty old fixings had been put to great strain in the storm. Now they could no longer hold him up. He tumbled to the ground and lay there while the cockerel, the hens and the

chicks pecked and scratched around him.
And the moral of the story is: You're no
use to anyone if you wear yourself out!

21

The Travelling Companion

Once there was a young man called John, whose family sadly all died. He did not want to stay at home alone, so he set off into the world to see where the road would take him.

As evening fell on the first day of his travels, the weather turned dreadfully stormy. John slipped inside a little church to take shelter. There before the altar was an open coffin and in it lay a dead man, waiting to be buried the next day. John wasn't at all frightened. He was sure that dead people can't do any harm. It was living people that he was more worried about.

John gave a coin to light a candle, then knelt and prayed for the stranger – that God would forgive his sins and welcome him into heaven. Then John settled down in a corner and spent the night there, keeping the dead man company.

Early next morning, John set off once

more. He had just strode through a forest when he heard a man call from behind. "Hey there, friend, do you mind if I travel along with you?"

"Not at all," said John. The two men talked as they walked, and soon came to like each other very much.

They journeyed on for many miles, until at last they caught sight of a town, with a great palace in the middle.

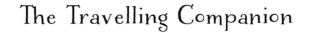

John and his companion did not enter the town straight away. First they stopped at an inn, to wash and change into clean clothes.

The innkeeper told them that the king was a good man, but his daughter, the princess, was an evil witch. She had declared that any man might try to win her hand in marriage. All he had to do was guess what she was thinking about. If he knew the answer, he would be her husband. But if he didn't know the answer, she muttered a wicked spell and he vanished, never to be seen again!

The innkeeper explained that sadly, hundreds of young men had disappeared in this way. The king was deeply upset about it, but his daughter's powers were so strong that he could do nothing to stop her.

Just then, John and his companion heard people shouting "Hooray! Hooray!" outside the inn. They hurried to see what was happening. The princess was passing by – and she was so beautiful that everyone forgot how wicked she was and cheered her!

John could scarcely catch his breath, he was so stunned by her. "I must go to the palace and see if I can win her hand in marriage," he decided. "Surely it can't be true that she is a wicked witch!"

The innkeeper and John's travelling companion both tried to persuade him not to go, but John would not listen. So the next day, the travellers walked to the palace.

The king was very sorry to see them, for he did not want John to vanish, like all the other young men. But John would not be put off. It was arranged that he would visit the palace again the following morning to guess what the princess was thinking of. And John fairly skipped for joy back to the inn, thinking only of how lovely the princess was.

As night began to draw in, the travelling companion brought John a glass of beer. "We must drink the health of the princess!" he said. But once John had had only a few sips, he felt so sleepy that he sank down over the table, snoring. Then John's friend opened the window. Wings suddenly sprouted from his shoulders and he flew off over the rooftops to the palace, where he perched on a ledge outside the princess's bedroom window.

At a quarter to twelve the window opened and the princess flew out. She had grown wings too! John's travelling companion made himself invisible, so he could follow her.

The princess soared away to a high mountain. She knocked on the mountainside and, with a rumble like thunder, it opened up. In went the princess and in went the invisible travelling companion after her.

They entered a long corridor built of silver and gold. The walls were lined with flowers which had snakes for stems and flames for petals. Eventually, it opened up into a vast hall. In the middle was a throne made out of

bones, and on the throne sat an old, evil-eyed sorcerer. The princess sank low in a curtsey to him and he kissed her forehead. "Think of my golden crown," he instructed her, "the young man will never guess that. And when he fails, don't forget to send him straight to me, so I may eat him…"

The princess curtseyed again and set off home, flying through the night air.

But the travelling companion did not follow her straight away. Instead, he crept close to the sorcerer and yanked the crown from his head. Then away he flew, leaving the sorcerer howling in a fit of rage behind him.

Next morning, John presented himself before the princess, with his travelling companion at his side. As he stood, puzzling hard over what she could be thinking of, John felt his friend push something into his hand. John held out his hand and opened it – and there was the sorcerer's crown!

The princess turned chalk-white, but there was nothing she could do. He was right.

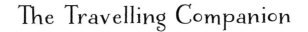

She sighed and said: "You are my master now. We will be married this evening."

That night, there was the most splendid wedding ever seen. Yet the princess scowled and was steely-eyed, for she was still an evil witch and had no love for John at all. When the festivities were coming to an end, John's travelling companion gave him a little bottle of liquid. "Put three drops in the princess's drink and then hold on to her tight," he said.

So that's what John did. To his astonishment, the princess turned into a black swan, struggling to get free. But John held tight and the black swan turned into a white swan, struggling even harder. John held tighter still – and then the white swan changed back into the beautiful princess. She was even more lovely than before!

Joyfully, the princess thanked John, for at last she had been freed from the sorcerer's spell which had made her so wicked.

The next morning, John's travelling companion wished him goodbye. "Your place is here now but I must move on," he said. "For I am the dead man you prayed for in church and now I have repayed your kindness." And with a smile, he disappeared.

Alas, John never saw his friend again, but he and the princess lived happily ever after.

The Snail and the Rose Tree

In a land far away, there was once a beautiful garden. It was surrounded by a hedge of hazel-bushes, heavy with hazelnuts. Beyond the hedge were fields and meadows in which cows and sheep grazed peacefully.

And in the middle of the garden a rose tree stood in full bloom. Under the blooming rose tree sat a tiny snail, thinking to himself.

"Just wait," he muttered under his breath. "One day I will show everyone! I will do much better things than grow roses like this tree, or bear nuts like that hedge, or give milk and wool like those cows and sheep."

"How exciting!" replied the rose tree. "I can't wait to see what you will do. Can I ask when you are going to do it?"

"Well, as you may have noticed, I take my time," remarked the snail. "The problem with you lot is you are always in such a hurry. You get on with things straight away, and then no one has anything left to look forward to!"

With that, he pulled himself inside his shell and refused to say a word more. Days passed by, then weeks, then months… and summer faded to autumn. The little snail crept deep

underground. The following summer, he crept once again into the dappled sunshine under the rose tree, and raised his head.

"Everything looks just like it did last year," he moaned. "Nothing has changed – the rose tree is still bearing roses, the same as before."

Again, the summer passed. As autumn arrived, the rose tree bowed its head and the snail crept back underground.

Then when spring began, the roses came out again – and the snail slowly came out too.

"You are an old rose tree now," the snail announced. "Why don't you hurry up and die? You have given the world everything you had – and I'm not sure that it was actually much use! How useful are roses, I wonder? Do you have anything to say for yourself?"

"Stop it! You are scaring me," said the rose tree. "I've never thought of things that way."

"You have probably never taken the trouble to think at all," scolded the snail. "Have you ever thought about why you bloom, and how it happens?"

"No," said the rose tree in a small voice. "I bloomed because I felt so glad. The sun warmed me and the air was so refreshing. I drank the dew and the cool rain. I felt power rising out of the earth and surging inside me, and energy from above flowing into my branches. I felt happier and happier – and so I went on blooming… That has been my life.

"Everything has been given to me," continued the rose tree. "But it seems as though nature has given even more to you. You always seem to be thinking so deeply,

37

you must have a very clever mind. I am sure
that one day you will astonish the world!"

"Astonish the world!" cried the snail. "I

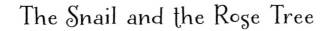

won't do any such thing! I am quite busy enough just thinking about myself."

The rose tree was quiet for a moment.

At last she said, "But shouldn't all of us be the best that we can, in order to help others? If you have been given such a clever mind, what are you going to use it for?"

"*What am I going to use it for?*" spat the snail. "I am not intending to use it for anything. You can go on bearing roses – it's what you're good at. The cows can give milk and the sheep can give wool – they all have people to please. But I want nothing to do with anyone – the world is nothing to me."

And with that, he withdrew into his house and closed up the entrance after him.

"How sad!" said the rose tree. "I could not creep into myself even if I wanted to. I have to go on growing roses. Then they drop their leaves and are blown away by the wind…"

And the rose tree went on blooming, while the snail lay lazily in his house, wanting nothing to do with the world.

Years rolled by and eventually, the snail crumbled into the earth – and the rose tree too. In the garden, other rose trees bloomed, bringing happiness to many other people. And other snails crawled about, creeping into their houses and seeing nothing at all.